# KNIT WITCH

## THREE SHORT STORIES AND THREE KNITTING PATTERNS

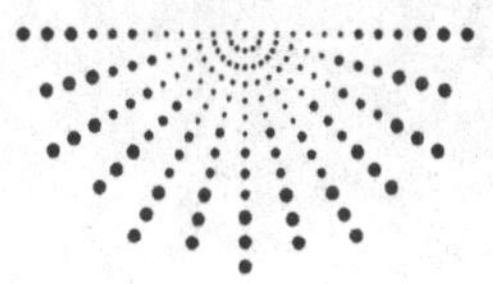

## STEPHANNIE TALLENT

For more information, contact: stephannie@stephannietallent.com

First e-Book edition January 2022

ebook ISBN: 978-1-942655-35-0
Print ISBN: 978-1-942655-36-7

www.stephannietallent.com

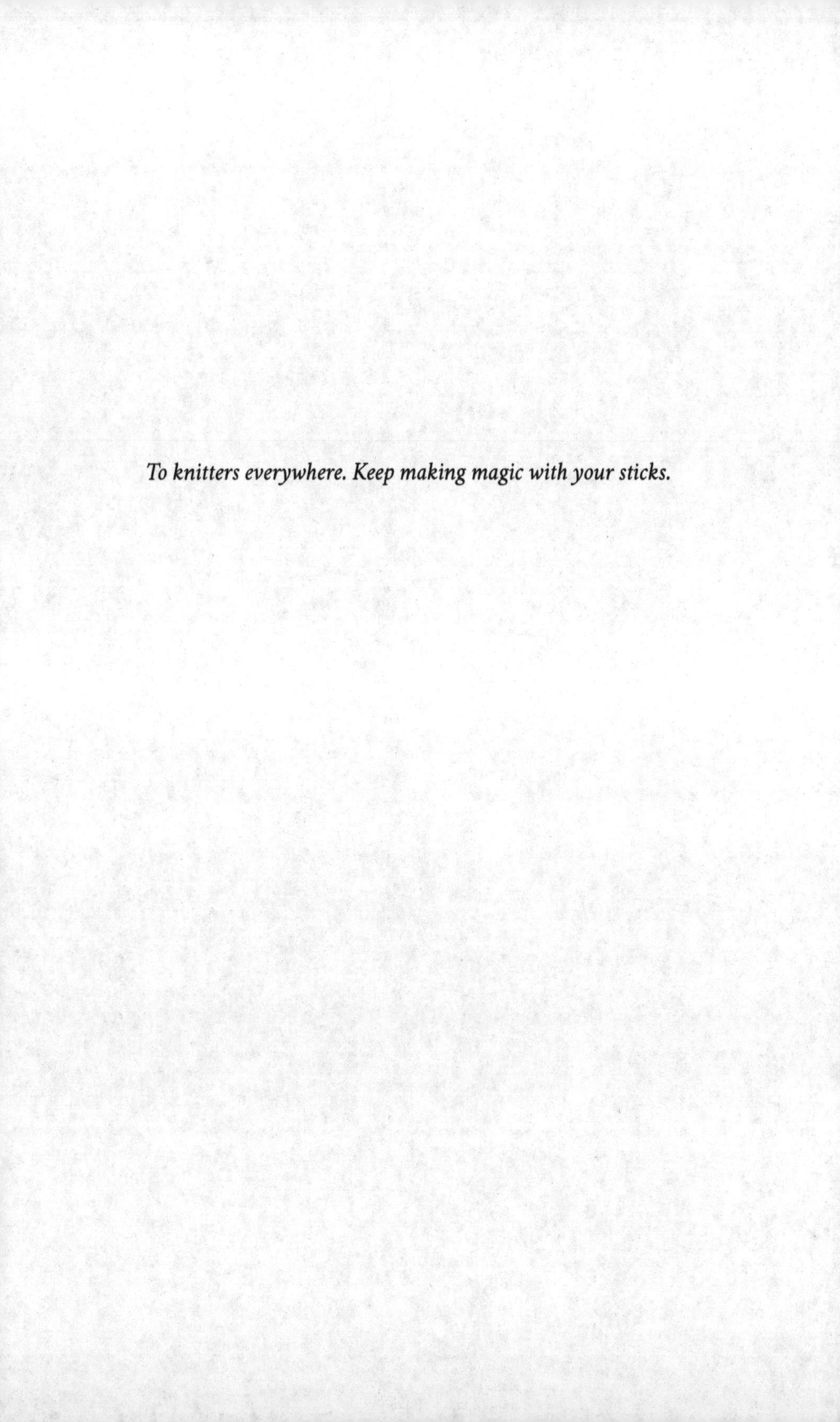

*To knitters everywhere. Keep making magic with your sticks.*

# CONTENTS

# INTRODUCTION

When you think about it, just the act of manipulating two needles and some string and making a hat, or a scarf, or mittens, is magic in itself.

Us knitters know that.

Three short stories and three knitting patterns round out this collection, featuring Janie, a knitting pattern designer, artist, and witch.

The patterns (two hats and a cowl) are suitable for beginning knitters comfortable knitting in the round.

If you like these patterns, please check out my knitting website, sunsetcat.com, for more patterns (and to sign up for my knitting email list).

# KNITTING HOPE

Hundreds of knitted panels, from the palest cream, to ivory, to mahogany, to the deepest inky black, all the colors of human skin, fluttered from the kinetic sculpture hanging from the Bridges Gallery ceiling. Rainbow stripes bordered the edges of some of the panels.

Fans directed an oscillating breeze, adding to the beautifully chaotic interplay of the panels.

Pre-opening jitter couldn't overcome Janie's love of the installation. But from here out, her opinion didn't matter.

The public's opinion did.

At least for Janie's pocketbook, lean after a disappointing holiday season.

Some panels featured textured stitch patterns, some lace, others intricate cables. The fibers ranged from precious gleaming silk, light soft merino, and even cloudlike cashmere, to nubby, sturdy hemps, linens, and cottons. At three feet tall by two feet wide, each panel was knit up of nearly enough stitches to make a sweater.

At least a short-sleeved sweater, or a tank top, depending on the size.

Janie adjusted the lighting, a combination of track lighting and recessed lighting, focusing it on the panels and dimming it throughout the gallery otherwise. She turned on the music app to her selected playlist, a mix of different ethnic folk music from around the world, then lit soy candles on carved wooden holders at each corner of the gallery. Scented with pungent rosemary and sharp mint, the candle fragrance wafted around the room with the eddies of air from the fans.

And she yanked on the strand of yarn at the end of a small knitted swatch, unknitting, or *frogging*, it swiftly, letting the stitches pop free.

She mentally directed the released magical energy to the base of the kinetic sculpture. It shivered in response.

She'd frog a bigger swatch right before the gallery opened.

Her panel was the moonlight pale one made of a linen/merino yarn, the stitch pattern a complex combination of airy lace and sturdy cables. Delicate beaded fringe, the hollow silver beads light as feathers, danced and clicked in the breeze along the bottom edge. She'd braided some of the same beads into her hair, in plaits cascading down her back.

Janie heard steps behind her, the sharp tap of heels on the rough unfinished wooden planks of the floor. The gallery was housed in a 1920s refurbished Spanish bungalow, nearly all the interior walls removed to create the main gallery space. The old oak floors had been too water-damaged to restore, and had been replaced with reclaimed panels from an old dairy barn in Sonoma.

"It's lovely," Kinsey, the gallery owner, said, picking a piece of cat fluff off Janie's shirt, then resting her hand on Janie's shoulder.

Kinsey was tall and elegant, wearing a magenta wool pantsuit tailored within an inch of her life, four-inch black crocodile stiletto open-toed pumps, and a bulky fused glass pendant, shot through with daggers of violet, fuchsia, and mustard yellow, crafted by her glass-artist niece. Kinsey's sleek black hair was pinned up in a deceptively simple knot.

Kinsey's outfit was in direct contrast to Janie's undyed hemp poet's blouse, embroidered flared jeans, and leather flip flops. And, apparently, cat fur.

Janie always felt scruffy, rather than her preferred Bohemian, next to Kinsey.

Kinsey's dark eyes narrowed. "A year's worth of work, and well worth it. Did you do a panel for me?"

"That one," Janie said, pointing to a dark ivory colored silk textured panel, with a rainbow border that scintillated in the adjusted gallery lighting. "No-nonsense, strong, but beautiful." The panel danced around Janie's in a delicate harmony, then continued to move around other panels.

"How does the movement work?" Kinsey asked, squinting up at the delicate contraption of slender rods and joints from which the panels hung.

"Mike programmed it," Janie said, and added to herself, *and I've magicked it*. Her biggest, and most difficult, working to date. Not that she could tell Kinsey that. Kinsey had no idea Janie was a witch, and would only scoff if Janie told her.

Her magic was slow and steady. She knitted her magic, and though she was one of the speediest knitters she knew, knitting was still an inherently slow way to craft spells. Even the tiniest charm swatch, just a few inches tall, a few inches wide, could take twenty minutes to knit up. Knitting built up the spell, and frogging the knitting (rip-it, rip-it, the sound of the stitches unraveling) released it.

The bigger the spell, the bigger the piece, the more time involved. And, frankly, more achiness from the repetitive motion, and even a bit of blood and pain, from the sharp tip of the needle hitting the same spot on her fingertip and gouging a hole as she pushed her work along.

Let alone the time she'd accidentally stabbed a knitting needle into the top of her foot. A boostered tetanus shot, and two weeks of antibiotics ... she still had the scar, five years later, from where she'd yanked the needle out.

With this installation, though, she hoped to harness the power of her spells through the movement of the pieces, rather than the destruction of them.

She didn't think that one little art show in a gallery in Oakland would make much of a difference for world peace. But maybe, just maybe, the interplay and harmony of her panels could reflect throughout the neighborhood, bringing together people of different races and beliefs in harmony, not anger or distrust. And maybe, the people touched by it could carry those thoughts and emotions elsewhere in their lives, and touch others.

You had to start somewhere.

———

THE EXHIBIT OPENED the next day to a modest but gratifying number of attendees. Kinsey always did a good job with the press, getting notice out to all the local outlets and papers, even getting a radio interview on the local NPR station for Janie.

Or maybe they were there for the free Prosecco and Trader Joe's cheese. Knitting (and its even less revered stepsister, crocheting) was often looked down upon as a mere craft by other artists.

Janie didn't care. People were there, mesmerized by the interplay of the panels, subconsciously swaying to the music, calmed by the scented candles. And smiling, and starting to talk to each other, not just with the friends they came with, but strangers chatting.

It was working. She watched the shadows of the people cast against the white plaster walls of the gallery. The shadows met, danced, then spun apart to interact with other shadows. Just like her panels.

She heard Kinsey's heels tap tapping on the floor behind her. Janie didn't know how Kinsey managed in her stilettos on the rough wooden floor; shoot, Janie tripped at least once every visit to the gallery, sometimes twice, even in her flip flops or cowboy boots.

"Janie, my dear, I'd like to introduce you to someone," Kinsey said as Janie turned to meet her. Kinsey wore tangerine wool today, and a fiery opal necklace, along with four-inch royal blue patent stilettos. She stood out like a flame against the panels.

Next to her was an older white man, dressed in a navy suit, crisp white shirt, a surprisingly flamboyant tie embroidered with peacock feathers, and black loafers. He had thick dark brown hair, just turning to silver at the sideburns and top, and a sun-weathered face, with crinkles at the corners of his light blue eyes.

He examined Janie in turn. Janie didn't know what he'd think of her tight boot-cut jeans and turquoise cowboy boots, or of her hand-knit indigo-dyed wool and cotton tank top, featuring the same stitch patterns as her panel in the exhibit. Probably not much. He looked like a stockbroker, maybe, or a Silicon Valley Angel. Not someone who would actually want to meet the artist, especially a young woman who could cosplay Morticia.

"Thomas Daniels," he said, holding out his hand.

"Janie Sullivan," she replied, shaking his hand. Thomas, not Tom. Yes, definitely, a *feel* of wealth, accompanied by the faint scent of tobacco leaves, leather, sea spray, and whiskey.

He was a walking embodiment of old money further focused by ambition. And a presumption of artistic flair, based on that peacock tie of his.

"Sullivan doesn't seem exotic enough for all this," he said.

"Sorry my name's not boho enough for you," Janie said evenly.

"Mr Daniels was at another exhibit earlier, purchasing for his office, and was walking past here on his way to dinner," Kinsey said, glaring at Janie. "Your installation caught his eye."

Janie looked past them. The shadows on the wall weren't moving as smoothly as before; they were bunching aggressively, then leaning away from each other, then separating. Not good. She didn't know if the shadows were responding to her agitation, or something else.

"Whose exhibit were you at earlier?" asked Janie. She'd *try*, try to be social. Rent to pay, cats to feed.

"Leroy Steadman's, down at the Fixx and Merritt Gallery," Daniels replied. "Abstract mixed media and oils. Incredible. I bought three pieces for our boardroom."

"Definitely unique with a strong viewpoint," Janie said.

He held out three postcards, each featuring a different abstract painting. "I purchased these."

Janie detested Steadman's work nearly as much as the man himself, having first met both five years prior. She suspected he worked magicks with his paintings—dark and painful spells. His work featured violent red, orange, and black jagged abstract patterns clawing and rending the canvas below.

The paintings flat out scared her.

Even the postcards Daniels showed her, just small reproductions, featuring the same sort of vicious red and black vision of his previous work, scared her.

Plus, Steadman had laughed at her at the opening of her first solo five years prior.

She'd created a series of crocheted and knitted coastal California landscapes, from vibrant orange crocheted poppies covering the knitted hills of Montaña de Oro State Park, to foggy wisps of fiber entwined with the Golden Gate Bridge, to crocheted sea urchins and starfish populating an underwater knitted view of La Jolla Cove. She'd worked in spells of wonder and protection, awe and sanctuary, and had collected thousands of dollars in donations to coastal conservation groups from visitors.

He'd laughed. Patronized her, dismissed her hard work and diligence of nearly a year as *pretty*, while looming over her from his six-foot-six height, appraising her through his tortoise shell horn rims, flexing his muscles under his tight fitting suit jacket, just daring her to stand up to him.

She'd come up with the perfect retort.

At home, laying awake in bed, near tears, two hours after the gallery had closed.

She'd taken care to avoid Steadman and his work since then.

If Daniels was a fan of Steadman's work, she couldn't understand why he'd even glanced at her installation.

"I believe we have a very different view of what our work as artists should be," Janie continued, directly to Daniels. She could see Kinsey out of the corner of her eye, throwing up her hands with their perfectly manicured and polished nails, rolling her meticulously made-up eyes.

"I can see that," Daniels said. "Your work is positive, hopeful. His is aggressive and destructive."

Janie barely stopped herself from recoiling. "Then why—"

"Did I purchase paintings from Steadman? I want that aggression to fuel my staff, when we're doing business deals. Your work, however, could bring balance, promote good will, after the deals are completed. Kinsey mentioned that you might be able to create smaller versions, smaller panels, for purchase later?"

How much did he know, how much did he believe, in magic? She didn't like that he would even use something like Steadman's work, that she felt was outright malignant, but a small part of her appreciated the irony of her work directly healing what Steadman's damaged.

And she and her cats Mae and Cary needed to eat. She had to make some money.

The shadows and panels were coming together again, tentatively at first, then with more assurance, pale shades flitting around the darker ones.

"Yes, I'll have smaller pieces for sale," she said. "You can contact me through the gallery. I actually have some smaller pieces nearly ready to go at my studio."

"Fabulous," Daniels said. "I'll be in touch. Kinsey, thank you for introducing me to such as talented and wise young artist."

"My pleasure," Kinsey said, escorting him to the gallery door. Janie saw her hand Daniels a card before he left; he handed her the postcards, which Kinsey tucked into the incoming-mail wire basket hanging off the wall just next to the front door.

Someone came up behind her and grabbed her in a bear hug. Pine and sea salt made her nose twitch. Mike.

"Hi, Mike," she said, relaxing back against him, the top of her head fitting neatly under his chin. "It works great, don't you think? Thank you so much for doing the coding."

"Man, how'd you know it was me?" he said, kissing the top of her head then letting her go.

She turned to face him. "You smell good," she said. He smelled like late spring on the seaside face of Mount Tam, that time the two of them went camping. She'd never been camping before, and was amazed at how much she loved it: campfires, s'mores, the swath of the Milky Way across the night sky, shielded from the lights of San Francisco.

His grandparents both sides were hippies from the Haight-Ashbury days, and his parents both yuppies, rebelling against *their* parents. He blended the two as a nature-loving, Mavericks-surfing, Silicon Valley software genius, a blond-haired, blue-eyed, All-American handsome tan cliché of every surf movie ever made since *The Endless Summer*.

"I may have a commission," she continued. "We can adapt the program for something with less pieces, right?"

"Super easy," he said. "A commission already? Awesome."

The panels danced merrily.

"And how are you holding up?" he asked. "Energy-wise?"

Mike was her dearest friend. Kinsey had remarked acerbically what a pretty couple, sunlight and moonlight, they made, after that camping trip, but their relationship was purely platonic. He knew what she was trying to do, the spells she'd entwined into each stitch.

"Perfect," she said. "There's no drain at all, the motion is fueling the panels, just as we planned. We'll have to hook up little battery powered motors for the commissioned pieces, rather than relying on plugging them in, though."

"No problemo," he said, and Janie laughed.

---

THE REST of the opening went well, better than Janie had even hoped. More people filtered in, even up until 10:30, a half hour after Kinsey'd planned on closing the gallery. And many requested info on buying smaller versions, or even just panels. One person, visiting from Chicago, even expressed interest in showing her work, including this installation, there.

Afterwards, Mike walked Kinsey the half mile to her rental, an old Craftsman bungalow that had been left alone for so many years it still had all its original features. Janie loved the warm wooden molding, the pocket doors, the beat-up old oak floors. She didn't care it had tiny closets in the two bedrooms (one bedroom for sleeping, one for her office slash studio), or beat up white tile kitchen counters, or a five by seven bathroom with an old dinged-up tub.

It had character.

Her kitties, Mae West and Cary Grant, littermates she'd adopted as abandoned strays, were happy to see them, weaving between Mike and Janie's legs as Mike uncorked a leftover bottle of Prosecco he'd snagged from the gallery.

Mae was a flamboyant calico with kelly green eyes, all sass and swagger, with a brash meow she wasn't afraid to use when she wanted something. Cary was an elegant tuxedo cat with white paws and a black mustache across his white muzzle, who usually perched up high, front paws crossed, surveying the world with a cool humor.

Mike had brought her tuberoses earlier in honor of her opening. Not much to look at, but they smelled heavenly, their heavy scent permeating her bungalow.

They shared half the bottle, then Mike left with a chaste kiss on Janie's forehead.

Janie, balancing nervous energy from the installation and sheer mental and physical exhaustion, drank one more glass of Prosecco. She changed into PJ bottoms and a soft cotton tank, washed her face, then went to bed, dreaming of knitted panels morphing into people and dancing, dancing, dancing.

———

SHE WOKE LATE the next morning, 9 a.m., well past her usual early wake up time of 5:30, with confused memories of her dreams turning to smoke and sirens.

Her cell phone was vibrating frantically. She always kept the ringer off, preferring outside communication to be on her schedule.

A dozen new text messages, three voicemails, all from Kinsey. Janie glanced at the texts first.

CALL ME ASAP
CALL ME
LISTEN TO VM
EMERGENCY CALL ME
And so on. She felt nauseated.
All caps? Kinsey never, never panicked.
She played the last voice mail listed.
Kinsey's voice, sobbing, shrill.
*The gallery burned down last night—*
Janie yanked on sneakers and ran out the door.

———

A HALF MILE isn't far, but Janie felt like she was in one of those dreams where, no matter how hard you ran, how fast you flailed your arms, how hard you gulped in air, you just weren't moving forward.

Finally she reached the Bridges Gallery. Housed in a refurbished 1920s Spanish bungalow, it had stood by itself on its tiny lot, and Janie guessed that was a mercy, because the only thing left was a pile of smoking rubbish, the singed fairy-light-wrapped Saguaro cacti from the desert landscaping in the front yard, and the surrounding three foot tall stucco wall. Even the wooden front gate, carved by one of Kinsey's artists, must've caught an ember, because it too had burnt.

Kinsey sat on the stucco wall, staring at the pile of burnt material. Broken red tiles from the roof. Wire mesh, melted into crumbled balls, from the gallery's stucco exterior. The smell, charred wood, chemicals from the firefighters, made Janie gag.

"It was insured, of course," Kinsey said dully, not even looking at Janie. "But that doesn't really matter. It's gone. The building had been here since 1921, did you know that?"

Janie nodded even though Kinsey was turned away. A tear trickled down Kinsey's face.

"The police think it was arson," Kinsey continued. "That the fire started in the main room. I'm so sorry about your panels, Janie. They were insured too, but they're like the house. Irreplaceable."

She finally turned to look at Janie.

"Good lord, Janie, what are you wearing?"

Janie hiccupped, looked down at herself. "My pajamas."

"Aw, now, aren't you cute," a deep baritone voice said. "Kitty-cat printed pants. And my, that tank top fits you well."

Leroy Steadman was walking down the street towards them, all muscle-bound six foot six of him, his gaze drinking in Janie's petite figure without shame.

"Sorry about Bridges," he said to Kinsey. "It was such a nice little place." His pale blue eyes were mild through his horned rim glasses, but Janie seethed at the malice dancing at the back of those eyes.

She hated him, she knew she shouldn't hate anyone, but oh, she hated this man.

And she knew he had something to do with the fire.

"Sometimes things just happen," he said to Janie. To Kinsey: "I'm sure the community will pull together and Bridges will be back one way or the other soon enough. Let me know if I can help in any way. A show to raise funds, pointing some of my clients your way, whatever I can do."

"Thank you, Leroy," Kinsey said.

"Janie, may I have a word with you?" asked Leroy.

She wanted Mae's claws, to shred his face. She needed Cary's composure. She drew on her love for her dear cats to strengthen herself. Her belief in goodness. Her love for Kinsey and Mike.

"What, Steadman?" she said.

"Walk a bit with me."

They walked down the block towards downtown, past other bungalows, some Spanish, some older Craftsman, all restored as small businesses: salons, galleries, restaurants. Thankfully, all of them were safe.

Steadman's long stride, even with him walking slowly, left her scrambling to keep up.

She hated him. *Hated* him.

"Hate?" he said. "Don't you believe that will just come back at you?"

"I don't care," she spat. "I know you burned down the gallery."

He stopped, looked down at her. "Of course I did. But there's no proof, no physical evidence the police can tie to me, because I magicked it. Remember those postcards I gave to Mr Daniels? He had no idea I was keeping tabs on him. Imagine my surprise when he went to Bridges." Steadman smiled. "Those postcards are ash now."

"Why?" she said. "Why would you?"

"Destruction, baby. Gotta feed the flames. And I don't like competition." He smirked, ran his finger along her cheek. She jerked away. "So what are you going to do about it, girl?"

She stared at him. "Fight," she finally whispered, tilting her head back to stare him straight in the eye. "Because I believe in hope. And hope doesn't die that easily, and it doesn't back down from a righteous fight."

She shoved past him, then ran back to the ruins of Bridges.

She had work to do.

# KNITTING OUT THE SORROW

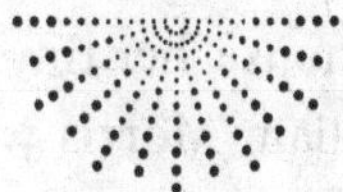

Janie sat cross legged on her beat up leather couch, counting stitches, counting on her knitting to heal her broken heart.

She was a witch, and crafted her spells through knitting. Maybe she could subliminally craft a spell to ease herself.

Her project was a simple Gansey patterned hat, a new pattern she'd designed that morning. Knit and purl diamonds would form a raised textured pattern against the rest of the fabric. She sat the hat-in-progress down to pick up her favorite handmade ceramic mug. Shaped like a fat friendly sheep with black wool, the mug contained her favorite Egyptian Licorice herbal tea.

The tea didn't taste like licorice or fennel. It tasted sweet. A bit of spiciness. Warming. Comforting.

She needed a little bit of comfort right now.

Not because of her knitting. Her knitting was fine. Shoot, she could knit, and even knit in easy spells of warmth and protection, in her sleep.

But last Friday...last Friday, a project she'd poured her heart and energy into, as well as her friend Kinsey's gallery, Bridges, had burnt down.

She regretted the loss of the gallery, the prettiest little Spanish Bungalow Janie had ever seen, more than her work.

She could re-create her installation. That bungalow dated from 1921. People didn't even use the same building methods or materials. The plaster walls that reflected sunlight just so, the coved ceilings....her heart broke again just thinking about it. Kinsey had loved that building so much. Put so much of herself into it.

The past couple days Janie barely left her couch.

She hadn't left her own house, her tiny Craftsman cottage with its smooth oak floors and William Morris wallpapered walls and wavy glass windows that welcomed the morning sunlight, at all.

It was just today, Wednesday, that she could bring herself to knit. Play music that didn't sound like a dirge over her blue tooth speaker. Eat more than canned soup.

Cary, her debonair tuxedo cat, trotted up to the couch. Chirruped. Floofy calico Mae sashayed into the living room, gave a guttural throaty mer-ow, and jumped up next to Janie.

"I know, guys, I know," Janie said. "I'm starting to function again."

That wasn't quite true. She'd been a dervish Saturday, helping Kinsey clean up, contacting her own insurance company, and Kinsey's insurance company. Serving as a point of contact for all the offers of help. Brainstorming potential fundraisers.

She functioned on overtime on Saturday.

Sunday it hit her, and she turned inwards. Monday was as dingy and dull as the fog swaddling her neighborhood of old Craftsman and Victorian houses. Tuesday brightened a bit, the sun burning the fog off.

Wednesday the sky was bright blue and the golden sunlight lit her living room.

This morning she felt she could knit and imbue the work with peace and hope, rather than fury and despair.

Start small. A hat spelled to keep someone less fortunate warm and safe, at least for a night or two. Then it would just be a normal hat. Made with love and good intentions, but not special in any other way.

Start small, now, but she had to learn to do *more*. If only she'd had a way to imbue the pieces in her installation with wards strong enough to resist the fire. To save the gallery. To create a spell that would really last.

The yarn, plump Cormo wool, dyed a chocolate-flecked tawny ecru like chocolate chip cookie dough, was a gift from her best friend Mike. He'd brought it by Sunday, and though she'd clung to the skein like it was a teddy bear, she hadn't wound it into a ball til this morning. The soft wooliness reminded her that someone loved her. Believed in her.

She'd gotten the ribbing done and was working on the diamond patterns that would decorate the main part of the hat. The thick wool was soft and springy against her hands. She could knit just by touching it, counting stitches under her breath. She could see the Cormo sheep, grazing happily. Smelled the green herby scent of the dew-touched grass as they chewed, felt the warmth of the late morning sun on her back. Noted the Great Pyrenees, pink tongue lolling as it kept careful watch, keeping them safe.

Janie smiled.

*That ewe was going to have a hard birth. She'd have to sleep in the bar, keep an eye on her. Twins. She'd likely be bottle raising one.* Someone else's thoughts—thoughts! —stabbing into her brain.

*Who the hell are* you?—an excruciating blast of awareness, as they noticed *her. Get out of my head!*

And Janie fainted.

———

SHE WOKE to Cary licking her cheek. When she opened her eyes, his face was about two inches from hers, his green eyes intent. The morning light had shifted to afternoon, and the living room was dim. She checked her cell phone. She'd lost several hours.

"I'm fine," she told Cary. But she didn't feel fine. She'd had flashes of clairvoyance before, but never, never telepathy.

And never felt so drained from an inadvertent use of power.

She drank the rest of her now-cold tea, then padded to the kitchen.

She was starving. Food before more tea. Friends had dropped off a bag of chicken and green chili tamales, a loaf of nutty banana bread, a plate of chocolate chip cookies. She devoured a cookie, then heated a couple of tamales in the microwave. She unwrapped them and ate them standing up. The chili zapped her taste buds with savory heat, and she thought of eating one more, but she felt steadier. More in control.

Instead, she called Mike.

"Hey, babe!" he said. Ever the surfer dude. Despite being a coding genius in Silicon Valley.

"Hey you," Janie said. "I started a new pattern with that yarn you got me."

"Awesome! What are you making?"

"A hat," she said. "I'm going to hunt down the label, but can you tell me a bit more about the yarn?" She knew he'd tried, when he dropped it off Sunday, to tell her all about it, but she couldn't hear him, couldn't bear his irrepressible Golden Retriever bounciness.

"Sure. I got it at the farmer's market. New vendor. Has her own herd, contracts out the processing to a small mill."

Mike, for all his perkiness, was dead serious about his diet and working out. He surfed the big waves at Mavericks; his life depended on his physical prowess, as well as a bit of luck.

So he knew every vendor at the small farmer's market, and what went into their produce. A new vendor would certainly catch his attention. Mike being Mike, he'd've stopped and chatted with a candlemaker or potter. But someone selling yarn? He probably went straight to them without even finishing his other shopping, knowing how much Janie would appreciate yarn from a local herd of sheep.

"Nice lady. Heather Tomasi. Cormo sheep, Sonoma County. We should take a roadtrip."

"Did you get any idea she might have powers? Magic?" She told him what happened earlier. Mike didn't have any arcane powers of his own, but he had assisted her with her installation, writing the computer code that created the movement of the different pieces in the installation, fueling the spells Janie had knitted in.

"Didn't pick up on anything, babe," he said. "But I grabbed her card for you, just forgot to give it to you Sunday. Let me take a pic and message it to you."

Her phone vibrated. "Got it," she said.

"Want me to bring by some take out for dinner? Seven-ish?"

She tested the idea. Interact with someone in person? She didn't flinch. Granted it was Mike, her best friend, but even yesterday she'd not wanted to see anyone.

Give her one more day, she'd be going out to eat. Walking around in public. Hitting a Starbucks. "Sure," she said. "Thanks. See you later."

Her brain started clicking, creating a to-do list.

Shower. Ugh, it'd been three days. Wash her hair, too. She felt greasy all over.

Straighten up the living room. Scoop out the litter boxes.

Call the woman on the card. Heather Tomasi.

———

MIKE SHOWED up a couple hours later, two grocery-sized brown paper bags in hand.

"Indian," he said, taking out a half dozen aluminum containers with cardboard tops and placing them on her butcher-block countertops. She could smell the curry and spiced yogurt.

She leaned in to stick a finger into the saag paneer and swipe some spinach.

"Back," he shooed her. "You're worse than Mae! Let me get it all out before you dive in. Glad to see you got your appetite back, though."

They ate in companionable silence. Chicken korma, butter chicken, saag paneer, shrimp biryani, and naan to wipe the plates. She'd have leftovers for a couple more meals. Mike wouldn't want any leftovers; tonight was enough of an indulgence.

They watched *Moulin Rouge* after cleaning up after dinner, snuggled up on the couch with an old blue striped afghan Janie had crocheted. Sunlight and moonlight, their friends always joked. Big rangy quintessential surfer dude Mike, all thick blond hair and sky blue eyes and beachy tan, and petite Janie with her pale skin and long dark hair and Bohemian vibe.

Janie was tucked up under his arm, feet curled under her. Mike sang along with most of the songs, not caring which character's song it was, male or female, belting them all out with gusto. Mae sprawled across her lap, enjoying Janie's absentminded strokes, and Cary sat up on the back of the couch where he could keep watch.

"Love. Above all, love," she murmured at the end. "I left a message for that woman earlier."

"Figured nothing had happened," Mike said. "Since you didn't say."

She picked up the hat-in-progress, running a length of yarn through her fingers. So soft. Warm. "The hat's coming along great."

He touched the raised up diamonds. "Make me one too? I like the pattern."

"Of course," she said. "But I could just teach you to knit, you know—"

*Breech. Get those rear legs into position. Pull on the hooves! Push, Coco, push! A gush of warm liquid. The second lamb was out. Felt its heart racing through its thin damp chest. The first lamb, sturdier, stronger, already nursing, its tail a pinwheel as it suckled. Coco takes one sniff at the second lamb and nudges it away. Bottle baby most likely. Maybe she could get Coco to take the lamb after a few da—*

Janie braced herself.

*GET OUT OF MY HEAD!!!*

"Motherfucking SHIT!" Janie yelled, then thought back, as hard as she could: *I'M NOT DOING THIS ON PURPOSE!*

She slumped against Mike, feeling like she'd thwacked the back of her head against, well, something hard. It hurt to think.

"I got smacked again. I'm not even trying to eavesdrop, and I think that's what that person thinks I'm doing," she said. She told Mike what she'd heard.

"Ouch. At least you didn't pass out." He shuddered. "All that baby birthing goo."

She picked up her cell, dialed Tomasi's number. No answer. She hung up.

"She's probably still out in the barn," Mike said. "You think it's her, right?"

Janie stroked the hat. "Maybe. Probably. A link through the yarn?" She had literally slept with that yarn, with the skein snugged up under her chin, smelling the faint scent of lanolin even in her sleep, every night since Sunday night.

Her phone thu-thumped its tiki drum ring.

"Hello?"

"Are you the idiot who keeps spying on me?"

"Are you the idiot who keeps giving me a headache?"

Silence. Then a snort of laughter. "Fair enough. I take it this isn't on purpose."

"Not for this bad of a headache, no." Janie paused. Shrugged. All in. "I'm Janie Osaka. Santa Cruz. Yarn artist and knitting designer. Witch."

"Heather Tomasi. Shepherdess and cheese maker. Witch," the woman, Heather, replied. "Since we're being all honest."

"I have some of your yarn," Janie said. "I think it's the reason why I reached you."

"Santa Cruz, hm?" said Heather. "I think this is best discussed in person. You're not too far. Fancy a road trip?"

———

THEY REACHED Heather's farm early the next afternoon, timing the drive to miss Bay area traffic as best they could.

Heather's yellow-painted farmhouse, a simple wood house that looked like an eighty year old grandma who was still strong enough to run marathons, nestled at the base of a small, oak-dotted hill. The house had a front porch with two huge wind chimes attached to the eaves at either end and a couple comfortable looking wooden chaises.

Thick grasses filled the rest of the barbed-wire fenced in property.

Fat fluffy sheep grazed happily, watched over by a spotted llama and a big white dog.

A two-story, weathered wood barn with a peaked tin roof was behind the farmhouse, as well as a couple livestock trailers and a stack of hay bales. Two pickups, one a glossy red Dodge Ram, the other a vibrant turquoise, vintage fifties Ford, sat on the gravel road that ran up to and around the house. Mike parked his SUV, a black Tesla, next to the pickups.

The air was cool, with a remnant of marine layer, that thick close cloud layer spawned by the sea, touching the hilltops to the west. The Pacific wasn't too far away, Janie guessed. Bodega Bay. Tomales Bay. Too far to pick up any briny smells, though. All she could smell was crushed grass and sheep, soon as she got out of the car.

And goat. Billy goat.

Nothing against goats, she liked goats, but their cheese tasted like they smelled. Not something she wanted in her mouth.

The wind chimes on the porch clonked.

A woman came out, letting the white-painted screen door shut behind her. She was tall and angular, with straw-colored straight hair tied back in a ponytail. She wore faded jeans, a black tank top, and a worn navy corduroy shirt. Her face was deeply tanned. She looked to be in her late 40s, but with that amount of sunshine, who knew.

"Thought I heard you drive up, though those Teslas can be sneaky," she said. "Heather Tomasi. You guys hungry for lunch?"

The living room of the farmhouse was cluttered but clean, filled with bags of cleaned fleece, yarn samples, and two different high end spinning wheels that Janie recognized from her own visits to her local yarn shop, their warm woods gleaming in the sunlight streaming through the uncurtained front window. A plush worn couch, slipcovered in a navy and white Japanese print fabric and a simple coffee table (with bowls of full of fiber samples and balls of yarn), two spindle-legged worn pine chairs, and an old oak, glass-fronted lawyer's bookcase were the only pieces of actual furniture. There wasn't room for any more.

Heather led them through the living room back to the dining

room. An old 1950s maple table and more of the pine chairs filled it. She'd already set the table, a vase of daisies in the center, for lunch.

"Tea okay?" she asked.

Janie and Mike nodded. They should have brought a bottle of wine, Janie thought. Something.

"I have cheese sandwiches and salad," Heather said, returning with the pitcher of tea, pouring it into their glasses.

Janie desperately hoped it wasn't goat cheese.

Heather arched an eyebrow. "Nope. Sheep, though. That okay? And sorry, but you were thinking that really really hard. Couldn't help but hear it. Let me get the food, we can eat, and we can talk."

The sandwiches, sharp cheese similar to Manchego, with arugula and fig jam, tasted so good Janie shared half of a second one with Mike.

"So what happened to you, kiddo?" Heather asked. "I can pick up the misery without even concentrating."

"Empath?" Janie asked, and Heather nodded.

"One of the reasons I'm happier out here in the boonies," Heather said. "Minor thought sensing as well."

"My friend's gallery burned down. Was burned down," Janie said. "I know who's responsible but I can't do a damned thing. Not yet."

"I'm so sorry. I did hear about that. Bridges in Santa Cruz. And you are the artist whose work was destroyed."

Janie nodded. "It was a working," she said, voice tight. "To help people really see each other, understand each other. Mike helped, he was key in me figuring out how to keep it powered.

"I need to learn more. Figure out how I can keep something like that from happening again. But it's not just that, it's all my working. Ephemeral." She fished the hat-in-progress out of her bag, a leather tote that was roomy enough to hold even a sweater's worth of knitting, along with her wallet and phone. "See? This hat, I'm knitting in extra warmth, protection. But that will only last a night, keyed by the person's wish. Then it's just a hat."

"A very nice hat," Heather said. She touched it. "That's the yarn your silent friend purchased. Coco's fleece from last year. She did accept the second lamb, by the way."

"That's good," Janie said. "About the lamb. But I was thinking, it was this yarn, me being with it, that let us accidentally link together. And I was wondering, if we did something *purposeful*, that I could somehow use the yarn itself, not just the action of my knitting, to power my spells."

"I love and raise these animals, nurturing each individual," Heather said. "They produce fine wool for me in return. I can't ask anything more of them. Perhaps, if I manipulated their life force, channeled some into their fiber, I could help do what you wanted. But I won't. I won't hurt my animals."

"Oh, no, I didn't mean that," Janie said, blanching. "I would never ask that."

"Power requires sacrifice. I can feel how your joints ache, just the tiniest bit, from your work. Over time that will get worse. You may just think your power is fueled just by intent and calories, but it's not." She shrugged. "Having said that, we can all make our own choices. Any sort of work we pursue— and I mean work as a job, or avocation, not just a spellcasting—requires some sort of sacrifice. Emotional, mental, physical. Late nights. Early mornings. Time away from families or friends. But we determine if it's worth it."

"It's worth it to me," Janie said. "I'm trying to make the world a better place. I know that sounds idealistic—"

"—Cheesy," offered Mike, finally speaking up.

"—but it's true."

Heather considered her. "Do you know how to spin?"

———————

JANIE DIDN'T KNOW how to spin that morning, but by early evening she did, though her yarn was lumpy, with thin as a thread, tightly twisted sections followed by barely spun clumps of fiber.

"You'll get better," Heather said. "Practice. And once you can spin whatever you want, yarn of any diameter, without even thinking about it, you can spell as you spin."

"And then I've layered more power into the yarn. Into the fabric," Janie said.

Heather nodded. "Yep. You're still working with fiber. With yarn. It's not like metal, or stone, that will last ages unless purposefully destroyed. You may not gain much time, say, for your hat, but it's something. A month. A season. I'll send you home with a bag of roving, ready to spin. Come back in a couple months and I'll teach you have to fully prepare a fleece, from cleaning it to carding it so it's roving ready to spin. And maybe we can figure out something for dyeing it."

"Thank you," Janie said.

"And in the meantime, stay out of my head," Heather said. "Like I said, I'm out here to stay away from people, not get spied on." She smiled, pulled Janie in for a hug. "Now get on home and get to work."

———

JANIE FINISHED the hat late the next day. She called Mike. "Got a present for you," she said. "Wear it after surfing when you need to warm up."

"Wow, I wanted one, but it didn't have to be this one. Thanks!" he said, feeling the squishiness of the ribbed brim, running his fingers over the raised purl stitches forming the diamonds. He put it on, posed, on leg forward, hand on his hip.

"Adorable. But you know that."

He smirked, then asked, voice soft, "How are you doing?"

"It's not enough," she said after a moment. "I need more. But it's a start. I have a plan, now."

And with a plan, she could do anything. She just had to believe in herself.

# THE STORY OF THE SKEIN

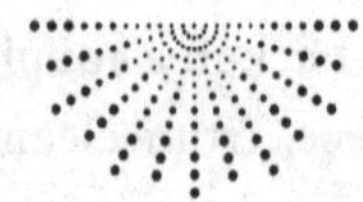

J anie fondled the skein of heathered brown yarn. Soft, so soft. And spongy, not silky. Cables. Braids and cables. They would just pop with this yarn. She checked the label for the fiber content: 50% yak, 50% cormo sheep. Made sense.

Then she smelled the yarn, a deep intake of breath of lanolin and hay that took her to the farm.

*Farms.*

Farms, plural.

The yak were from some place higher, colder, where their wool would grow warm and long. Colorado? That felt right. She could *see* snowy peaks and rich gray granite in the distance, feel the nip of high desert cold. A small herd of yaks, about ten of the dark shaggy beasts, their curved tan horns gleaming in the midmorning winter light, raised their heavy heads. Dark brown eyes regarded her for a moment, then they lowered their heads to graze on the dried winter grasses.

The fluffy Cormo sheep were just up the coast, north of Mendocino. Janie could taste the salty ocean air, feel the spray against her cheeks. The sheep looked like puffy clouds against the green winter pasture. They ignored her, except for one ewe, who baah'd at her, her strident voice ringing Janie's ears until Janie set the skein back into the sea grass basket filled with its fellows.

Yep. This yarn was *hers.*

She had a week to get the project done, a pattern promised to her friend Jess for Jess' online knitting magazine, but hadn't been able to pick a yarn from her own stash (two cedar chests' worth of yarn!) that called to her.

Oh, she could make do. But she really wanted something that spoke to her.

Something that would be magic, in her hands. Janie didn't expect to change the world, but every bit of good she could do, every bit of good others could do, added up. She had to believe that.

And as a fiber witch, she had the power to do good. And use it she must.

Her and Spider Man. Though her power was little, not great.

This last minute stop at the Santa Rosa farmer's market was her last chance to find the yarn that spoke to her.

This yarn did.

The yarn would bloom once she washed the final project, the yarn plumping out the stitches. The cables would be glorious and twisty and fat. It was perfect.

She gathered up three skeins from the sea grass basket. Enough for a hat and matching mitts, with enough left over for a pompom.

Twenty bucks a skein, but it was a tax write off, right? Janie did earn a sizable part of her income from her knitting pattern designing business, with patterns for sale on Ravelry and other sites.

"It was processed in an old fiber mill up north that just closed," the yarn seller, a short round older woman with oversized black framed glasses turning her amber eyes huge. "My specifications. Fiber I got from friends. Won't be able to make it again, I'm sorry to say."

"It's lovely," Janie said. Oak leaves. Oak leaves and cables. Janie's mind already ranging to the possibilities, she paid and headed to the bike rack at the far end of the market.

She'd biked from her apartment to the farmer's market. It wasn't far, just a couple miles, easy on her old beater bike, a hybrid with beat up red ripstop canvas panniers hanging on either side of the rear wheel. She tucked the skeins of yarn into one pannier and a bag of Fuji apples into the other, then pedaled out towards the main road.

She noticed the car ready to make a righthand turn into the market. Noticed the orange flash of the blinker.

Figured it was safe.

Rode into the street.

And that's all Janie remembered.

————

JANIE SHIVERED, hugged herself. She was still wearing the stretchy black yoga capris, black sneakers, and grey sweatshirt she'd left the house in that morning. But it wasn't enough for this high desert plateau, with the dusting of snow over juniper bushes. The sunlight was a washed out gray that just added to the cold and flattened everything, the bushes, the undulations of the frostbit ground. Shards of minerally ice cut into her nasal passages as she breathed in. The sharp peaks stabbing into the low hanging gray clouds seemed terribly far away, too far away to give any relief to the flatness.

Lost. Lost in an expanse of bitter cold. She clenched her fists, not even feeling her short nails dimple her palms.

Something grunted.

Behind her.

She scrambled to her feet, staggering as she turned, her feet blocks of ice in her sneakers.

A yak, moist broad nose just inches from her face, dark brown eyes inquisitive under its long forelock, grunted again, expelling warm air pungent with yak spit and grass. Frost dotted its long coat. Its smooth horns captured a bit of wan sunlight and gleamed, flashed, briefly, gold. It looked like a robust, very fuzzy cow.

It licked her, thick tongue swiping up from her chin to past her nose.

*Ewww.*

A second yak sidled up next to Janie, snugging up against her left side. A third nestled up to Janie's right side. Janie warmed up, enough to feel her fingers running through their thick coarse guard hairs to the downy undercoat.

Something trickled down her forehead. She touched her finger to it. Warm. Sticky.

Red.

"I'm bleeding," she told the yaks. They grunted and nestled closer.

*Feel the wind. Listen how it weaves and dances*, the first yak said, its warm voice vibrating inside her skull. It licked her face, her forehead.

Janie closed her eyes. The wind toyed at her blood-sticky bangs, lifting and separating the strands, then tangling them back together. She could feel the wind running through the coats of the yaks, weaving the hairs into thin braids and coils, then separating them, again and again.

*Let it knit your skin back together*, the yak said.

Janie relaxed against the yaks, eyes still closed. The wind tugged at her skin, the raw edges dulled by the cold, until the edges met and held tight.

*Remember us*, the yak said. *Remember the wind.*

"I will," Janie promised.

And the plateau tilted sideways.

———

NOT WARM. But warmer. And saltier. Janie opened her eyes.

A fat Cormo ewe stood in front of her. Her body was long, longer than she was tall, and her fur so dense that Janie, reaching up, could barely penetrate it with her cold fingers. She smelled like wet raw wool, of hay and lanolin and ocean dampness. She had a long bare nose and mild curious yellow eyes.

She baah'd, sheep spit spraying into Janie's face. *You again.*

"Yes, me again," Janie replied. It was the ewe she'd *seen* when she smelled the yarn.

*How does your head feel?*

Her brain was throbbing, now that the ewe brought Janie's attention to it. Pulsing in time with her heartbeat. Pressing against her skull with every breath.

"It hurts. I think there's swelling," Janie said.

*Damn yak should've fixed* that, the ewe grumbled. *The outside doesn't matter as much as the inside. Well, come along. I can help you do what's needed. Lean on me if you need to.*

Janie stood, legs shaking. Blood drained from her head to her feet and her legs felt like posts in an earthquake. What should be solid, wasn't. She rest her hand on the ewe's wooly back and walked, steps hesitant, with the ewe to the end of the pasture.

A barbed wire fence separated the edge of the pasture from the drop off to the ocean below. Waves, white with fury, pounded against the guano-tipped rocks below.

The world spun and rocked. Janie clenched the ewe's wool, cramping her fingers against the greasy warm plushness.

*It's called the Mendocino Fracture Zone*, the ewe said. *The earth moves here, relieving pressure all the time. I can feel it through my hooves, vibrating and trembling, I can feel it in my teeth.* She fixed her yellow eyes on Janie. *Sit, child, and feel the earth. Feel it move through your body, shifting to release all that pent up pressure.*

Janie crumbled to the rocky turf, keeping one hand against the ewe. The grass was cold and damp with ocean mist, but deeper, she could sense heat. Heat and friction and pressure, pressure that dwarfed that throbbing in her skull.

Pressure that raised mountain ranges and split the earth.

Janie breathed in. Out. Tried to match the movement of the faults, the long tail of the San Andreas, the Gordo plate, the Pacific plate, even the San Juan plate further north. Shifting under the ocean and reaching all the way east to Lassen.

Something *gave*, snapped, and the earth under her rolled and bucked.

*Yee hawwww!* bawled the ewe. *Ride it out, honey, ride it out and let it all go!*

Janie screamed and flattened herself against the grass, praying to all the goddesses she could think of that the top of the cliff didn't shear off and plummet into the ocean below.

But she listened to the ewe, all the same, and let the quake wash through her, letting everything relax, including the dreadful pressure in her head.

Until the edge of the cliff did crumble, and she fell.

————

*IT's time to spin it all together.* Weathered pine siding, warm gray in the late morning sun, creaked over the sound of machines clacking inside. *Come on in, witch, and see how it all comes together.*

A door, solid pine without windows, opened, and Janie walked on in. Her head felt fine, no horrible pressure, no blood dripping, but the whir and clack of the machines, combing wool into thick pencils of roving, then spinning the roving into strands, then twisting those strands together, echoed the rattling in her chest.

Dust rose from the machines and twinkled in the overhead fluorescent lights, hung from exposed scarred beams. So much dust she could taste it coating her tongue, acrid and vegetal all at once. The cavernous room smelled of wool and machine grease and sweat. People worked at every machine, making sure nothing got kinked up or tangled or stopped. It was a candy factory for a fiber witch for her, a candy factory based in the past.

"I thought the mill closed," Janie said.

*I'll still be here til the last bit of fiber from me gets eaten by a moth, or degrades in a landfill. Nothing lasts forever, but wool lasts a good long time,* swayed the lights overhead.

*Now watch, and see how it all comes together.*

At the far end, hot water streamed into big tubs. Whole fleeces soaked, hay and grass and muck all floating to the top of the water. Rinse, repeat, rinse.

The cleaned fleeces dried.

*Worsted yarn or woolen?* asked the mill.

"Woolen," Janie said, thinking of her cables. Worsted, or smoothly prepared yarn, would show her cables better than fluffier woolen yarn, but woolen cables had a rusticity that would suit her design.

*Let's get to picking and carding.* The fleece was separated into smaller pieces by one machine; the next machine further separated the fiber into a thin airy layer, a batt.

Broken down. The fleece was broken down. Her chest ached and tightened.

"I can't breathe," Janie whispered. Everything felt loose. Adrift. She tasted blood on the back of her tongue.

*Let's go on,* the mill said hastily. *Just a bit more, just through the condenser to separate the batt into slivers. Then we can rebuild. Hang in there, Janie.*

Ropes of airy fiber, the slivers, appeared. Janie panted and slid to the fiber dusted floor.

*The spinning frame is next. Twist! We'll add twist to the slivers. It's the foundation of the yarn. Hold on!*

"I don't think I can," Janie gasped. "It hurts so much."

The strands twisted. Yarn, if you wanted single ply.

The pain eased, just a little.

*Double ply, Janie, double for your cables.* Two strands met, and plied together, a strand of two ply yarn, wound into two hundred yard skeins. *There! See, Janie, I told you! It's broken down and remade.*

*As are you.*

And even as Janie gulped air, her chest expanding freely, everything went black.

———

"Just stay there, don't get up," someone said, and Janie squinted. The yarn seller, amber eyes owl-like behind her thick glasses.

"What happened?" Janie's tongue felt thick, fiber-dust coated in her dry mouth.

"You got hit by a car, honey," the yarn seller said. "Dumbass signaled but didn't actually turn. You looked pretty bad."

Janie bet she had. Her chest ached and her head throbbed, but even that was dimming, retreating. "I think I'm fine now."

"Just wait for the paramedics, okay?"

Janie nodded. She *knew* she was fine, but she didn't want to argue. "Your yarn."

"Your bike got messed up, but your apples and the yarn are fine."

"Saved my life."

The yarn seller laughed. "Well, I doubt that, honey, but I do believe there's a magic in well-made yarn. Promise to do something special with it, and I'll give you a couple more skeins for being such a tough young woman."

"I can do that," Janie said.

And she could. Would. A design that blended the wind with the earth and the endless motion of the mill.

She could do that.

# PATTERN NOTES (BOTH HATS)

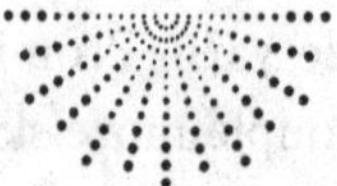

## GENERAL

These hats are worked in the round from the bottom up.

First work an optional tubular cast on, directions included, or your preferred stretchy cast on, in the following section, then proceed to either pattern.

## YARN SUBSTITUTION

The most important thing for substituting yarn is swatching and getting a blocked fabric that you like.
The closer you're able to get to the composition, fiber choice, and weight of the yarn of the pattern as written, the less variance in gauge, yarn usage / amounts, etc, will occur.

# BRIM (BOTH HATS)

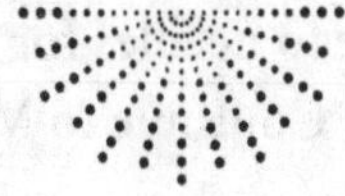

*I prefer working a tubular cast on for the brims of these hats (I love the rolled edge effect!) but wanted to include instructions for both a tubular cast on (or) your choice of stretchy cast on.*

## CAST ON, OTHER THAN TUBULAR CAST ON

With needles for ribbing, cast on 102 (114, 126) sts and join in the round, being careful not to twist. Pm for beginning of round.
Work 15 rounds of [k1, p1] ribbing.
Continue to Main Body.

## TUBULAR CAST ON

*I've experimented with various tubular cast ons, and prefer this one, modified from Brooklyn Tweed, best.*

Using waste yarn, and needle size one size smaller than for ribbing, cast on 52 (58, 64) st.
Set up Row (WS): Using yarn for project, purl all stitches.

Row 1 (RS): *K1, p incr, rep from * to last st, sl1 purlwise. *103 (115, 127) sts*

Join in the round, being careful not to twist, slipping last stitch of round from right to left needle wyib, pm for beginning of round.

Round 2: Sl2 purlwise wyib, p1, *sl1 purlwise wyib, p1, rep from * to end.

Round 3: K2tog, sl1 purlwise wyif, *k1, sl1 purlwise wyif, rep from * to end. *102 (114, 126) sts*

Remove waste yarn. Change to needles for ribbing and work [k1, p1] ribbing for 13 more rounds. Continue to Main Body section.

# JANIE'S DIAMONDS HAT PATTERN

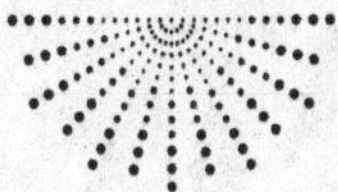

*This unisex slouchy hat features a center band of large seed stitch diamonds with bands of smaller purl diamonds above and below.*

*Use handpainted yarn for a colorful hat with hints of textures, or a solid yarn for more distinct patterns.*

*This hat is a companion to my short story, The Fabric of the Stitches. In that story, Janie works on a hat pattern while recovering from a horrible loss.*

*A variation, Janie's Chevron Hat, also available, features both chevrons and diamonds.*

## SIZES

Unisex S (M, L), to fit 20 (22, 24)" / 51 (56, 61) cm head circumference

## FINISHED MEASUREMENTS

Head circumference: 19¾ (21¾, 24)" / 50 (55.5, 61) cm
Height including brim: 9¼ (9¾, 10¾)" / 23 (25, 27.5) cm

## YARN

The Yarn Collective Pembroke Worsted, 100% merino wool (219 yds / 200 m per 3.53 oz / 100 g), 1 skein (143 (164, 195) yds / 131 (150, 179) m), shown in size small in Carnelian.

## NEEDLES

US 6 / 4 mm, or size needed to obtain gauge
US 5 / 3.75 mm, or one size smaller than size needed to obtain gauge, for ribbing
US 4 / 3.5 mm or one size smaller than needles ribbing, for tubular cast on
Your choice of circular needles or DPNs for working in the round

## GAUGE

22 sts and 32 rounds = 4" / 10 cm in St st with largest needles

NOTIONS

(6) stitch markers, (1) unique for beginning of round; yarn needle; waste yarn if doing tubular cast on; pom pom maker for optional pom pom

SKILLS

Working in the round, increases, decreases

INSTRUCTIONS

Work brim (see Brim section) then proceed to Main Body.

MAIN BODY

Change to larger needles.

Increase round: *K17 (19, 21) sts, m1, rep from * to end of round. *6 sts increased, 108 (120, 132) sts*

All sizes: Knit 10 rounds.

Note: Repeat, between **, is worked 9 (10, 11) times around.
Round 1: *[K3, p1, k2], rep from * to end.
Round 2: *[K2, p3, k1], rep from * to end.
Round 3: *[K1, p5], rep from * to end.
Round 4: Purl to end.
Round 5: *[K1, p5], rep from * to end.
Round 6: *[K2, p3, k1], rep from * to end.
Round 7: *K1, [k2, p1] 3 times, k2, rep from * to end.
Round 8: *K5, p1, k1, p1, k4, rep from * to end.
Round 9: *K4, [p1, k1] 3 times, k2, rep from * to end.

Round 10: *K3, [p1, k1] 4 times, k1, rep from * to end.
Round 11: *K2, [p1, k1] 5 times, rep from * to end.
Round 12: *[K1, p1], rep from * to end.
Round 13: *[P1, k1], rep from * to end.
Round 14: *[K1, p1], rep from * to end.
Round 15: *K2, [p1, k1] 5 times, rep from * to end.
Round 16: *K3, [p1, k1] 4 times, k1, rep from * to end.
Round 17: *K4, [p1, k1] 3 times, k2, rep from * to end.
Round 18: *K5, p1, k1, p1, k4, rep from * to end.
Round 19: *K1, [k2, p1] 3 times, k2, rep from * to end.


Round 20: *[K2, p3, k1], rep from * to end.
Round 21: *[K1, p5], rep from * to end.
Round 22: Purl to end.
Round 23: *[K1, p5], rep from * to end.
Round 24: *[K2, p3, k1], rep from * to end.
Round 25: *[K3, p1, k2], rep from * to end.


Next: Knit 2 (4, 9) rounds, placing markers every 18 (20, 22) sts on the last round. (If you want a taller hat than specified in the finished measurements, knit extra rounds at this point.)


## CROWN DECREASES

Crown decrease round: [K2tog, knit to 2 sts before marker, ssk, sm] to end of round.

Work crown decrease round initially then every 3rd round 7 (8, 9) times. *12 sts remaining*

Last round: K2tog around, removing markers as you work. *6 sts remaining*

Cut yarn, leaving a 6" / 15 cm tail. Thread yarn through live stitches and pull snugly to close hole at top of hat.

## FINISHING

Weave in ends. Block.
Make optional pompom if desired and attach.

# JANIE'S CHEVRON HAT PATTERN

*This slouchy unisex hat, with or without the optional pompom, is all about texture and comfort.*

*The seed stitch chevron and diamonds pattern is enough to keep your interest, and to show off the lovely yarn, but isn't too complicated.*

*This hat is a companion to my short story, The Fabric of the Stitches. In that story, Janie works on a hat pattern while recovering from a horrible loss.*

*This is a variation of her first version, Janie's Diamond Hat.*

## SIZES

Unisex S (M, L), to fit 20 (22, 24)" / 51 (56, 61) cm head circumference

## FINISHED MEASUREMENTS

Head circumference: 19¾ (21¾, 24)" / 50 (55.5, 61) cm
Height including brim: 91/4 (9¾, 10¾)" / 23 (25, 27.5) cm

## YARN

The Yarn Collective Hudson Worsted, 100% Merino Wool (219 yds /
200 m per 3.53 oz / 100 g), 1 (2, 2) skein(s) (186 (214, 261) yds / 171
(196, 239) m), shown in Size Small in Natural.

## NEEDLES

US 6 / 4 mm, or size needed to obtain gauge
US 5 / 3.75 mm, or one size smaller than size needed to obtain gauge,
for ribbing
US 4 / 3.5 mm or one size smaller than needles ribbing, for tubular
cast on
Your choice of circular needles or DPNs for working in the round

## GAUGE

24 sts and 36 rounds = 4" / 10 cm in St st with larger needles

## NOTIONS

(4) stitch markers, (1) unique for beginning of round; yarn needle; waste yarn if doing tubular cast on

## SKILLS

Working in the round, increases, decreases

## INSTRUCTIONS

Work brim (see Brim section) then proceed to Main Body.

## MAIN BODY

Change to larger needles.
Increase round: *K17 (19, 21) sts, m1, rep from * to end of round. *6 sts increased, 108 (120, 132) sts*

All sizes: Knit 1 round.

Note: Repeat, between **, is worked 9 (10, 11) times around.
Round 1: *K5, p1, k6, rep from * to end.
Round 2: *K4, p3, k5, rep from * to end.
Round 3: *K3, [p2, k1] twice, k3, rep from * to end.
Round 4: *K2, p2, [k1, p1] twice, p1, k3, rep from * to end.
Round 5: *K1, p2, [k1, p1] 3 times, p1, k2, rep from * to end.
Round 6: *P2, [k1, p1] 4 times, p1, k1, rep from * to end.
Round 7: *[P1, k1] 5 times, p2, rep from * to end.
Round 8: *K1, p1, rep from * to end.
Round 9: *[P1, k1] twice, p2, [p1, k1] 3 times, rep from * to end.

Round 10: *K1, [p1, k1, p1] 3 times, k1, p1, rep from * to end.

Round 11: *P1, k1, p2, k3, p1, [p1, k1] twice, rep from * to end.
Round 12: *K1, p2, k5, p2, k1, p1, rep from * to end.
Round 13: *P2, [k3, p1] twice, p1, k1, rep from * to end.
Round 14: *P1, k3, p2, rep from * to end.
Round 15: *K3, [p2, k1] twice, k2, p1, rep from * to end.
Round 16: *K2, p2, [k1, p1] twice, p1, k3, rep from * to end.
Round 17: *K1, p2, [k1, p1] 3 times, p1, k2, rep from * to end.
Round 18: *P2, [k1, p1] 4 times, p1, k1, rep from * to end.
Round 19: *K1, p2, [k1, p1] 3 times, p1, k2, rep from * to end.

Round 20: *K2, p2, [k1, p1] twice, p1, k3, rep from * to end.
Round 21: *K3, [p2, k1] twice, k2, p1, rep from * to end.
Round 22: *P1, k3, p2, rep from * to end.
Round 23: *P2, [k3, p1] twice, p1, k1, rep from * to end.
Round 24: *K1, p2, k5, p2, k1, p1, rep from * to end.
Round 25: *P1, k1, p2, k3, p1, [p1, k1] twice, rep from * to end.
Round 26: *K1, [p1, k1, p1] 3 times, k1, p1, rep from * to end.
Round 27: *[P1, k1] twice, p2, [p1, k1] 3 times, rep from * to end.
Round 28: *K1, p1, rep from * to end.
Round 29: *[P1, k1] 5 times, p2, rep from * to end.

Round 30: *P2, [k1, p1] 4 times, p1, k1, rep from * to end.
Round 31: *K1, p2, [k1, p1] 3 times, p1, k2, rep from * to end.
Round 32: *K2, p2, [k1, p1] twice, p1, k3, rep from * to end.
Round 33: *K3, [p2, k1] twice, k3, rep from * to end.
Round 34: *K4, p3, k5, rep from * to end.
Round 35: *K5, p1, k6, rep from * to end.

Next: Knit 3 (5, 5) rounds, placing markers every 27 (30, 33) sts on the last round. (If you want a taller hat than specified in the finished measurements, knit extra rounds at this point.)

## CROWN DECREASES

Crown decrease round: [K2tog, knit to 2 sts before marker, ssk, sm] to end of round.

Work crown decrease round initially, then every other round 6 (7, 7) times, then every round 5 (6, 7) times. *12 (8, 12) sts remaining. Remove all markers (except beginning of round marker) on the the last decrease round.*

Last round (S and L only): K2tog around. *6 (8, 6) sts remaining.*

Cut yarn, leaving a 6" / 15 cm tail. Thread yarn through live stitches and pull snugly to close hole at top of hat.

## FINISHING

Weave in ends. Block.
Make optional pompom if desired and attach.

# MICACEOUS COWL

*Although not part of the Janie stories, this cowl pairs well with either hat,
depending on color and simple knit/purl stitches for the fabric.
The biasing caused by the increases and decreases of the chevron pattern has
an interesting effect on the square blocks in this unisex cowl, tilting them into
a pattern reminiscent of three-dimensional illustrations of boxes.*

## SIZES

S (M, L)

## FINISHED MEASUREMENTS

Height: 8 (8, 11¼)″ / 20.5 (20.5, 28.5) cm
Circumference: 21¾ (27, 59½ ) ″ / 55 (68.5, 151) cm

## YARN

Anzula Croquet, 50% merino, 50% tussah silk (230 yds / 210 m per
4.06 oz /115g); 1 (1, 2) skein(s) C1; 1 skein C2; 92 (114, 332) yds / 84
(104, 304) m C1; 40 (51, 167) yds / 37 (47, 153) m C2.
Shown in Watermelon (C1) and Avocado (C2) in size m.

## NEEDLES

US6 / 4 mm, or size to obtain gauge
Gauge
18 sts and 27 rounds = 4″ / 10 cm in pattern stitches (blocked)

## NOTIONS

Minimum (1) stitch marker for beginning of round, yarn needle

## SKILLS

Working in the round, increases, decreases, changing colors at beginning / end of rounds

## PATTERN NOTES

This cowl is worked from the bottom up in two colors as noted in the stitch patterns.


## STITCH PATTERNS

Chevron pattern (repeat of 12 sts and 11 rounds), worked in C1
Round 1: Knit.
Round 2: Purl.
Rounds 3, 5, 7, 9: [K1 tbl, k2tog, k2, kfb twice, k3, ssk] to end.
Rounds 4, 6, 8, 10: Knit.
Round 11: Purl.


Block pattern ((repeat of 12 sts and 11 rounds), worked in C2
Round 1: Knit.
Rounds 2-10: [K6, p6] to end.
Round 11: Knit.


## INSTRUCTIONS

Cast on 96 (120, 264) sts in C1. Join in the round, being careful not to twist. Pm for beginning of round.
Work each stitch pattern repeat 8 (10, 22) times around, placing stitch markers between repeats if desired.


**All sizes**
Work chevron pattern in C1.
Work block pattern in C2.
Work chevron pattern in C1.
Work block pattern in C2.
Work chevron pattern in C1.

**Additionally, for size large *only***
Work block pattern in C2.
Work chevron pattern in C1.

**All sizes**
Bind off as follows: *K2tog tbl, slip stitch to left hand needle, repeat from * to last unworked stitch on left hand needle, k2tog tbl.

FINISHING

Weave in all ends. Block.

# KNITTING PATTERN ABBREVIATIONS

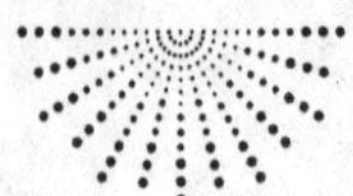

C1: color 1 (chevron pattern for cowl)

C2: color 2 (block pattern for cowl)

k: knit

k2tog: knit two stitches together

kfb: knit into the front of the stitch, leaving the stitch on the needle, and then knit into the back of the same stitch

p incr: lift the horizontal strand between stitches with the tip of the left needle inserted from front to back. Purl into the front leg.

p: purl

p2tog : purl two stitches together

pm: place marker

rep: repeat

RS / WS: right side / wrong side

sl: slip

sm: slip marker

ssk: slip two stitches knitwise, then knit slipped stitches together through the back loop

st st: stockinette stitch

st(s): stitch(es)

tbl: through the back loop
wyib: with yarn in back
wyif: with yarn in front

# ABOUT THE AUTHOR

Since graduating from West Point, Stephannie Tallent has served in the Army as a Military Intelligence officer during Desert Storm, gotten a Zoology degree, went to vet school, worked as a small animal veterinarian, and designed and published knitting patterns and books.

Throughout all that she's always wanted to be a writer, and she's finally put all her type A, soft-spoken, invisible middle-aged woman focus on that goal, writing everything from fantasy to science fiction, mysteries and romance.

She has sold stories to **Pulphouse Magazine** and the **WMG Holiday Spectacular**.

www.stephannietallent.com

Sign up for Stephannie's newsletter!
https://www.stephannietallent.com/subscribe/

# ALSO BY STEPHANNIE TALLENT

*Short Story Collections*

Gates of Wonder

The Chronicles of Dinah Lee Wright Vol 1

The Chronicles of Dinah Lee Wright Vol 2

Gratitude of the Ocean: Jolene Tomberlin Series

The Serpent in the Shallows: Jolene Tomberlin Series

The Monkey's Journal

The Kaleidoscope Jaguars of the Jungles of Mexicatl

The Mermaid of Ellis Prime

The Alchemy of Science and Mystery

One Plus One Equals More (mystery/crime)

A Snowman Made of Sand (romance)

KnitWitch (fantasy and knitting patterns)